AMERICANS

To my family.
And to every American striving to create a more perfect Union
—D. W.

For my grandparents who, many years ago, made their way to this country.
And for my father, whose service in the US Army during WWII helped keep America free.
—E. S.

☆ ☆ ☆ ☆ ☆

SIMON & SCHUSTER BOOKS FOR YOUNG READERS
An imprint of Simon & Schuster Children's Publishing Division
1230 Avenue of the Americas, New York, New York 10020
Text copyright © 2018 by Douglas Wood, Inc.
Illustrations copyright © 2018 by Elizabeth Sayles
All rights reserved, including the right of reproduction in whole or in part in any form.
SIMON & SCHUSTER BOOKS FOR YOUNG READERS is a trademark of Simon & Schuster, Inc.
For information about special discounts for bulk purchases, please contact Simon & Schuster Special Sales
at 1-866-506-1949 or business@simonandschuster.com.
The Simon & Schuster Speakers Bureau can bring authors to your live event. For more information or to book an event,
contact the Simon & Schuster Speakers Bureau at 1-866-248-3049 or visit our website at www.simonspeakers.com.
Book design by Laurent Linn
The text for this book was set in Minister Std.
The illustrations for this book were rendered in acrylic paint on Arches Watercolor paper.
Manufactured in China
0418 SCP
First Edition
2 4 6 8 10 9 7 5 3 1
Library of Congress Cataloging-in-Publication Data
Names: Wood, Douglas, 1951– | Sayles, Elizabeth, illustrator.
Title: Americans / Douglas Wood ; illustrated by Elizabeth Sayles.
Description: First edition. | New York : Simon & Schuster Books for Young Readers, 2018. | Audience: K to Grade 3. | Audience: Ages 4 to 8.
Identifiers: LCCN 2016000756| ISBN 9781416927563 (hardcover) | ISBN 9781481452366 (eBook)
Subjects: LCSH: National characteristics, American—Juvenile literature.
Classification: LCC E169.1 .W72 2018 | DDC 973—dc23 LC record available at http://lccn.loc.gov/2016000756

AMERICANS

Douglas Wood

Illustrated by Elizabeth Sayles

Simon & Schuster Books for Young Readers
New York London Toronto Sydney New Delhi

WE THE PEOPLE called Americans differ from one another in many ways. But despite the differences, Americans share certain ways of doing and being that hold us all together.

Lincoln Memorial, Washington, D.C.

Americans love.

We love our ideals of human dignity and freedom. We love liberty, the opportunity to pursue happiness, and all the promise the future may hold. We love our families, neighbors, and friends.

7

Totem Pole (Tlingit) of the Pacific Northwest

John Muir

NATIONAL PARKS

Americans especially love the beauty of their land: oceans that sparkle, crash, and sing; green blankets of forests that drape the hills; sunny prairies under endless skies; white-shouldered mountains and hidden valleys; and great gouges of

Golden Gate Bridge, San Francisco, California

Grand Canyon, Arizona

Everglades National Park, Florida

canyons that reach down to the beginning of time.

Americans know that all these things are gifts to be cherished and protected, and passed on to future generations of Americans.

Background: Grand Teton National Park, Wyoming

Americans create.

Never have a people tried so hard to find a "better way," creating so many things that weren't there before: a lightning rod; a cotton gin; a steamboat; a sewing machine; an airplane; a typewriter; a telegraph; a telephone; a television; an elevator; a phonograph; a spaceship; a computer; a cell phone; a laptop; the Internet.

Betsy Ross sewing the first American flag.

But greatest of all, over two hundred years ago Americans invented a new country and a form of government—the modern democracy—that has inspired the world.

Mark Twain using one of the first typewriters

Robert Fulton's first steamboat on the Hudson River, New York

President John F. Kennedy

Telephone poles stretching across the country

11

Amelia Earhart

Empire State Building construction workers, New York, New York

12

Jackie Robinson

Reverend Martin Luther King Jr.

Sonia Sotomayor

Americans dream.

We know we are lucky to live in a land where people have the freedom to try, to fail, and to succeed; where hard work is rewarded; where people can climb as high as their hearts and minds can reach.

The history of America is full of people who tried, and tried again, who struggled and fought the odds, who kept going in the face of disappointment and discouragement, and who finally achieved great and worthy goals. Their stories are why we are here today.

Background: Orville and Wilbur Wright testing an airplane near Kitty Hawk, North Carolina

Americans believe.

We believe in a good greater than ourselves. We believe in one another. We believe that people should be free to believe—in whatever truth their heart holds dear, so long as their belief harms no one else.

Bill of Rights
FIRST AMENDMENT

Congress shall make no law respecting the
establishment of religion or prohibiting the free
exercise thereof, or abridging the freedom of
speech, or of the press, or the right of the
people peaceably to assemble and to
petition the government for redress
of grievances.

Pueblo eagle dancer

VOTES for WOMEN

To Struggle to Right the Wrongs

One thing Americans do especially well is disagree.

We disagree because human beings are different and unique, and everyone has different eyes for seeing the world. Americans are free to disagree—with politicians, with organizations and religions, with their own government. Even Americans who disagree, agree on the freedom *to* disagree.

But Americans still come together to help one another, to forgive one another, and to work for the one goal we all share: creating a better country.

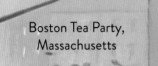
Boston Tea Party, Massachusetts

Background: Great Depression soup line

RICAN
CROSS

Americans care.

We share with others, with friends, relatives, neighbors, and people we don't even know. Americans help people who are less fortunate and in need of a helping hand.

Americans know that the entire country can be strong and whole only if all its members are strong and whole. But Americans also look far from home, to lands and peoples around the world, and ask, "What can we do to help?"

TUSKEGEE AIRMEN

We Can Do It!

Rosie the Riveter poster from World War II

Background: Revolutionary War drummers

Sometimes Americans fight.

We are fierce fighters when we defend important ideals like human dignity and freedom.

Americans may fight because our country has been wounded or attacked, and must be defended.

Other times we have chosen to fight for people who are weak or wounded, poor or bullied, and unable to defend themselves. In such cases, many Americans have sacrificed their own lives in order to help.

But Americans also make peace.

We try to create a more peaceful world, for our own families and for families of other lands. Many parts of the world are now more prosperous, safe, and free because Americans helped.

United Nations headquarters, New York, New York

USA

USA

My name is

USAID Foreign Education Assistance

Background: WWII Aid Drop

USA

23

Americans make mistakes.

Like all people, we are not perfect. We were not perfect in the past, and we will not be perfect in the future. But Americans keep reaching for perfection, keep trying to create "a more perfect union," keep trying to do better, to be better.

E PLURIBUS

President Abraham Lincoln signs the Emancipation Proclamation

Japanese internment camp during World War II

Cleaning a polluted river

Background: Dust Bowl of the 1930s

By the People

Freedom of the Press

the CONSTITUTION

Freedom of

President George Washington

President James Madison

Benjamin Franklin

For the People

Freedom of Religion

Speech

Freedom of Assembly

LIBERTY
for
ALL!

In this constant effort to reach
a little higher, Americans grow.

We grow from roots that are very deep and very
strong. It is from these roots that the great, living tree
called America grows. And although the tree may bend
in the wind, its roots remain firmly planted.

the BILL of RIGHTS

Americans choose.

We have the power to make important, personal choices in our daily lives. We may choose to change—to change our jobs or careers, to change religions or political parties, to change leaders or the direction of our country.

Americans know that only by allowing choice can our country be kept free.

Background: The Oregon Trail

Americans hope.

It is perhaps the thing that Americans do best of all. We have hope for ourselves and for our country. We believe in the possibility of improving so that our children and their children will live in a better country and world than we do now.

"Give me your tired,
your poor, your huddled
masses yearning to breathe free,
the wretched refuse of your teeming
shore. Send these, the homeless,
tempest-tossed to me, I lift my lamp
beside the golden door!"

—*Emma Lazarus*

And we, the people who
love it, are called Americans.

Fourth of July fireworks at the U.S. Capitol building, Washington, D.C.

In 1865 when the Civil War was over, Congress passed the Thirteenth Amendment making all slaves *legally* free. Finally, all men were considered equal under the law.

Japanese Internment Camps during WWII

When Japan bombed Pearl Harbor, Hawaii, in 1941, America was left with no choice but to officially enter World War II. Many people of Japanese ancestry lived on the West Coast, and some Americans became suspicious of their loyalty. Could they be spying for the Japanese Empire? These American citizens were rounded up and put in internment camps (a kind of prison) until the war ended. During this time, they lost their livelihoods, their homes, and their freedom.

Kids celebrating Earth Day by picking up trash

Earth Day began in 1970 as a way to focus attention on the problem of pollution. Celebrated annually on April 22, many people pick up trash, remove plastic bottles from streams, and many other activities to save and protect the Earth.

PAGES 26–27:

Spots:

George Washington

So deeply did George Washington want America's freedom from Great Britain that he became a general in the Revolutionary War. Despite being one of the Founding Fathers, he did not sign the Declaration of Independence because he was still out on the battlefield. Washington was elected as the first president of the United States in 1789, and served for two terms.

James Madison

James Madison, our fourth president, earned the nickname "Father of the Constitution" because of his work on both the Constitution and the Bill of Rights. He made sure the Constitution included a system of checks and balances, which ensures that no one person gains too much power in the federal government.

Benjamin Franklin

Benjamin Franklin was a jack-of-all-trades. He was a scientist, an author, a diplomat, and a statesman. It was Franklin who started the first lending library in America. He knew that citizens needed to be educated if they were to be involved in the democratic process. Franklin also signed of the Declaration of Independence.

PAGES 28–29:

Background:

Wagon train traveling West

Americans have always had the right to choose the path they wanted to follow, and the open spaces out West seemed to offer endless opportunities. Some very determined citizens went all the way to California when news reached them that gold had been discovered there. Although some got rich quick in the short-lived Gold Rush (1848–1852), the majority of those going west settled along the way and became farmers or ranchers.

PAGES 30–31:

Background:

Statue of Liberty welcomes visitors and immigrants to the U.S.

The Statue of Liberty was a gift from France in 1886 and has become a symbol of American freedom and democracy. Standing on Liberty Island in New York Harbor, the statue became a beacon of hope for immigrants heading to nearby Ellis Island. Although not every immigrant was granted entry to United States, over its many years of operation from 1892 to 1954, Ellis Island welcomed more than 12 million immigrants into the U.S.

PAGE 34:

Background:

Fourth of July fireworks at the Capitol in Washington, D.C.

The domed Capitol Building in Washington, D.C., was completed in 1800 and has served ever since as the home of the U.S. Congress and the seat of the legislative branch of the U.S. government.